The Potter's House

To Lou, may the Grace of
God always abide

[signature]

ISBN 978-1-64349-714-3 (paperback)
ISBN 978-1-64349-716-7 (digital)

Christian Faith Publishing, Inc.
832 Park Avenue
Meadville, PA 16335
www.christianfaithpublishing.com

Printed in the United States of America

The Potter's House

Philip Robinson

BACKGROUND scene: An old goblet, slightly tarnished with a few chips is sitting up on a shelf beside a small lump of clay (his grandson). They are looking at a table below filled with plates and table settings. To one side of the cupboard is a group of cups that are dazzling to the eyes. They are beautiful, sparkling under a single light seemingly just for them. If any other approached even close to them, they would shoo them away with a look of disdain.

Grandson: Grandpa, look at those beautiful cups over there. I've never seen anything so beautiful in my entire life. Who are they, Grandpa?

Grandpa: Oh, those, well son, those are the communion cups.

Grandson: Communion cups? What is a communion cup?

Grandpa: Those are the vessels that show up for a special occasion each month, specifically on the first Sunday.

Grandson: What's so special on that day, Grandpa?

Grandpa: On that day each month people celebrated the death and resurrection of the one who saved mankind.

Grandson: Oh, you mean, the Potter.

Grandpa: Yes, son, that's who I'm talking about.

Grandson: Do they come out any other time, Grandpa?

Grandpa: I'm afraid not, son. They consider their job done.

Grandson: I think that's a shame, Grandpa something that pretty and only being seen on one day.

Grandpa: Son, it is a shame.

Grandson: Grandpa, will I get to see him?

Grandpa: Who?

Grandson: The Potter, Grandpa.

Grandpa: You can bet your life on it.

Grandson: Ooooh, I hope I look like one of those cups over there. He'll be sure to pick me up.

Grandpa: You think so, huh? Maybe, maybe not.

Narrator: So the little bit of clay looked on the table as the dishes and utensils went about their chores for the feast that was to be given, thinking how great it would be to be picked up by the Potter if he was pretty and beautiful.

Grandson: Grandpa, why are those cups running around the table filling themselves up with water?

Grandpa: Those are the everyday cups. Their jobs is to quench the thirst of all who gather at the table to eat.

Grandson: Water, uhhhh, that's what makes us soft. I was told to stay far, far away from that stuff because it makes us weak and gooey.

Grandpa: Yes, son, it can. But only if it's not poured out right. See, we need some water because without it we can never be what we can be. We'll only be a dry piece of dirt.

Grandson: Grandpa, how much water have you had?

Grandpa: Lots, son, more than I can measure.

Grandson: Grandpa, did you ever leak? I hear old cups leak and have cracks.

Grandpa: Hey, watch you language. I don't leak, son, but I've spilled some in my day. Don't believe everything you hear in the cupboard.

Grandson: I'm sorry, Grandpa, but you know, there's talk around the table.

Grandpa: Son, that's okay. I've been around the table a few times, and I know the gossip. No offense taken.

7

Narrator: The feast is in full swing, and the cups are working in a frenzy to keep up with the demand for more and more refreshments.

Grandson: Grandpa, those cups are sure getting a workout tonight. They must have travelled a zillion, zillion miles and still everyone wants more. Don't they ever stop?

Grandpa: That's their job in life son, to bring a refreshing drink to those who are in need of refreshing.

Grandson: Grandpa, most of them don't have water in them. They have what's in those bottles with the pretty faces on them over there.

Grandpa: Oh, those.

Grandson: What's in them, Grandpa? Some of them are foreigners, but they are all related, I think.

Grandpa: Why do you say that, son?

Grandson: They all have the same last names, Grandpa.

Grandpa: Last names!

Grandson: Yes, Grandpa, 180-proof, 90-proof, even some little ones that say 2 percent.

Grandpa: Stay away from that group, son. They will fill you up with all kinds of bad stuff. By morning you won't know where you will wake up. When they are empty, they go out with the trash.

Grandson: You mean they go to the dark place, Grandpa?

Grandpa: Yes, son, that dark place, *the landfill.*

Narrator: The banquet is over, and the table is being reset for the next meal, and there are new clean plates on the table.

Grandson: Grandpa, I want to be a plate.

Grandpa: Why do you want to be a plate, son?

Grandson: Because they get all the good stuff that people like. See, all the good stuff is on them. Everyone chooses them first, not like us, we get picked last all the time—and when we have only water in us, a lot of times we are left full on the table. The soda, Kool-Aid, and those proof bottles get chosen before them.

Grandpa: And you think that's not fair, right? That makes you want to be a plate, huh? Getting all the choice things, but who is left holding the crumbs after the meal. Who is scrapped and ignored after everyone is full. Who is left holding the discarded food that sometimes is not even good enough to be given to the dogs.

Grandson: I didn't see all that, Grandpa. Grandpa, you're so full of smart things!

Grandpa: Some of the things seem glamorous at first son, but are thrown when they're of no more use. Remember that, son. In the good old days we knew what was in us. Pure clean water. Nowadays you don't know what they will pour into you next.

Grandson: I will, Grandpa.

Narrator: As they look at the table, Grandma enters the cupboard.

Grandson: Hi, Grandma. Grandpa was telling me about the good old days

Grandma: Yes son, as Grandpa was saying in those days you knew what you were getting. No funny labels, none of that foreign stuff with bugs in it. Ugggh. No XXX on it. Yes, those were the days.

Grandpa: The cups then knew what was in them. Nowadays you got to be careful. The label says pure, but pure what? When the top comes off, then you see what's really in them. Don't get fooled by the pretty outsides. It's what inside that counts. Some sweet, some bitter, some smell good, others not so good, some taste good, some only with a bunch of useless calories and additives.

Grandson: Grandma, can I get a *STAIN* when I grow up?

Grandma: A *STAIN!* Whatever do you want one of them for?

Grandson: Grandma, the new style is getting a *STAIN*. It's what all the young people are getting. Judy Jugs has a grape *STAIN* on her handle of her boyfriend Muggsy.

Grandpa: What is she going to do when she gets older and needs a job? Who will want to drink from her with that stain, huh, who?

Grandson: Ooooh, I never thought of that. Can it be wiped off?

Grandma: Sometimes, but it may take a lot of hard rubbing, or even chipping.

Grandson: Uh-uh, that hurts. I don't want to have to do that.

Grandpa: Sometimes the only way to remove some stains is painful. It may hurt.

Grandson: Grandma, see those pretty cups over there. Aren't they pretty?

Grandma: They are pretty, son, but looks aren't everything. Though they are pretty, what good are they to a thirsty person if something is only in them once a month?

Grandson: People would die, I guess. Right, Grandma? They wouldn't look so pretty then.

Grandma: You are absolutely correct, son. They would die of thirst, holding an empty cup.

Grandpa: Son, you're getting the picture. Ha, ha, the pitcher, get it?

Grandson: I get it, Grandpa. The Pitcher, Reverend Pitcher, right?

Grandson: Grandpa, can I be a pitcher?

Grandma: Maybe someday, but first you have to be able to hold just a little bit of water so the Potter can make of you what he needs most.

Grandson: Do you leak, Grandma?

Grandma: I've been known to spill a few drops in my early days. Oh, I was so eager to satisfy someone's thirst that I spilled the drink before I got to them. They went away still thirsty. I felt so ashamed. So you have to be careful. The water you may carry came at a terrible price, you know. The Potter's son was made a vessel and came down full of his Father to give us the everlasting water that never ceases. So every drop he gives us to quench someone's thirst is precious.

Grandson: Grandma said without the water we can never be molded into anything he can use, right?

Grandpa: Right, son, so right.

Grandma: So, son, without the water, we could not become the
vessels we are today. See, we were hard clay destined to
be thrown away. But the Potter knew if he could get just
a little water in us, he could mold us into a useful vessel.

Grandpa: Nowadays, they have all kinds of water to put into
us—sweet, sour, fruity, sporty, looks like clear but got
something else mixed in. But remember, it must still have
the essential ingredient—clean water. Yes, sir, no matter
what, you got to have the pure, clean, sweet water.

Grandson: Okay, okay, Grandpa, I get it. You don't have to lecture
me anymore. I get it. Grandma, I'm thirsty. Can I have
a soda pop?

Grandpa: Kids!

About the Author

Philip Robinson grew up in a small town in rural Maryland. He and his younger brother used to daydream lying on the hillside around their house. Philip grew up without electricity until the age of sixteen. The most exciting outlet he had was reading. The author entered the military after high school and eventually became an instructor, which allowed him to be more outspoken. This also encouraged him to be able to express himself more with words. As a Christian, he became fascinated with the word of God and the need to get kids enthused about God in a way that they would enjoy through dreaming and connecting with the Word of God. His wife encouraged him to put those thoughts on paper, which lead him to write this story. Philip is married to his wife of forty-three years, Cynthia, and they presently have four children, Philip J. Robinson II, Tangela, Brian, and Michael, and eight grandchildren.

Philip Robinson   205-728-7400
1359 chelsea Park Trail
chelsea AL
          35043

Printed in the USA
CPSIA information can be obtained
at www.ICGtesting.com
JSHW071737170823
46615JS00005B/34